Stories of Princes & Princesses

Christopher Rawson
Adapted by Lesley Sims

Illustrated by
Stephen Cartwright

Reading Consultant: Alison Kelly
University of Surrey Roehampton

Contents

Chapter 1

The clumsy prince

Colin was the clumsiest prince in the kingdom. Other princes fought dragons. Colin fell over them. Other princes battered villains. Colin bumped into them.

One day, he tripped in front
of a sad princess. She thought
he was so funny, she wanted
to marry him on the spot.

Her father had other ideas.
He gave Colin three tests, tests
he knew Colin would not pass.

First, Colin had to show how polite he could be. But he was so busy talking politely to the queen...

...that he didn't see the butler.

Next,
he had to
take the
princess
out. But
somehow,
he lost the royal boat.

Then he had to ride the royal
horse like a prince.

"He rides like a clown!" said
the king.
"He must
leave the
palace
tomorrow."

That night, Colin couldn't sleep. Suddenly, he heard a scream. It was the princess!

Help! I'm being kidnapped!

Colin jumped. What was going on? Was someone stealing the princess? He leaned out of his window and sent a flower pot flying...

...straight onto the head of the man stealing the princess.

The princess thief fell to the ground with a thud.

Colin raced from the tower and swept up the princess.

The king and queen raced out too.

"What's going on?" cried the king. "What has Clumsy Colin done now?"

"He's rescued me!" said the princess.

"Really?" said the king.

"Really!" she said.

The king smiled. "Well, the reward for rescuing a princess is to marry her," he said.

So Colin lived clumsily, but happily ever after.

Chapter 2

The princess who wouldn't get married

Prue liked being a princess, except for one thing. She didn't want to marry a prince.

"You have to," said her dad. "It's what princesses do."

The king asked three princes to visit. "Choose one," he told Prue.

But Prue didn't want to. "Princes are boring!" she said.

Prue did like the third prince. But she didn't say so.

Too hairy!

The king was angry.

If you won't marry a prince, you'll marry the first man who comes to the castle!

The very next day, a beggar
arrived, playing an old violin.

Prue and the
beggar were
married on
the spot.

With his beard, the beggar reminded Prue of someone. Whoever he was, she didn't want to marry him. But the beggar took Prue home as his wife.

"Cheer up!" he said. "If you married a prince, you'd have to live in a boring castle."

The beggar was kind, but very poor. They wore old rags and never had enough to eat. Prue was used to servants. Now, she did everything.

One day, the beggar brought home some straw.

"We can make baskets to sell," he said. But the straw cut Prue's hands.

"You must get a job," said the beggar. "Prince Alec is getting married. Perhaps you can work in the castle over the hill."

The castle cook was pleased to have help. She took pity on Prue and gave her some food.

Prue was going home when she passed the ballroom. She sighed. There was Prince Alec, giving a speech to his guests.

Perhaps it wouldn't have been so bad to marry a prince...

Just then, the prince turned around and saw her.

"You're the hairy prince!" cried Prue.

Prue tried to run away and the food fell from her apron. The guests began to laugh.

"I'd like to dance with you!" said the prince and he reached for her hand.

Prue
burst into
tears. She
pulled her
hand from

the prince and fled.

But Prince Alec caught up
with her. Prue looked at him
closely. It was her beggar.

Don't you recognize my violin?

24

He took her back to the ballroom.

"Would you marry a prince now?" asked Alec.

"I would," said Prue. "But I'm already married to you!"

Chapter 3

The princess and the pig boy

Once, a poor prince named Sam lived in a tiny castle. All he owned were a beautiful rose tree and a lovely nightingale.

Sam fell in love with a rich princess named Sara. So, he sent her his beautiful tree and the lovely nightingale.

But Sara was not pleased. "A silly tree and a noisy bird?" she said. "Send them back!"

Sam didn't give up. He went to Sara's palace and got a job taking care of the palace pigs.

But Sam missed his home.
He especially missed the
lovely songs of his nightingale.
So, he made a rattle which
played magical tunes.

Sara was out with her maids when she heard the rattle.

"I want it!" she said.

"It costs one hundred kisses," said Sam.

"Never!" said Sara. But she did want the rattle. "I'll give you ten kisses," she said.

"The price is one hundred," said Sam. Sara had to give in.

The king was on his balcony, when he heard giggling. It was coming from the pig sty.

What's going on down there?

The king hurried down. He crept up behind Sara's maids and looked over their shoulders.

The king was very angry.
"Princesses don't kiss pig
boys!" he shouted. "Both of
you must leave at once."

Go and never
come back!

Sam and Sara had to leave
the palace.

"I don't even like pigs," said Sara. "I wish I'd married that poor prince."

Sam quickly changed his clothes behind a tree. "You can!" he cried.

The poor prince!

The happy prince!

Sam took Sara to live in his tiny castle. Sometimes, she even watered the rose tree.

Chapter 4

The smelly prince

Percy was the rudest, dirtiest, smelliest prince in the country.

He lived all alone in his dirty old castle. He didn't like children. He hated animals. He had no friends, not one.

Even his soldiers called him Smelly Perce – though not to his face.

He was a very lonely prince, until one day, he had an idea. He would capture a princess and marry her.

Percy grabbed the first princess to come along. He was taking her home when they passed some moles. There were mole hills all over his field. Percy was very angry.

Percy locked the princess in a tower. But she had already agreed to marry someone else – a clean prince named Harry.

"I shall rescue her at once!" Harry said...

...but he couldn't get into Percy's castle.

Just then, a mole popped its head above ground.

"Percy smashed our homes," it said. "We'll help you."

Don't worry, your highness. We'll soon get you into the castle.

The moles dug all night.

They dug all of the next day too. By the following evening, they'd built a tunnel.

It ran all the way under the moat and into the castle.

Prince Harry was delighted. The tunnel took him into Percy's dungeons.

Harry set the prisoners free. Then he went to find Percy and the princess.

Percy tried to stop Harry. But his sword was so rusty, it bent. He was no match for Harry.

As if that wasn't bad enough, Harry's soldiers decided Percy needed a bath.

To Percy's surprise, he found being clean was fun. And people were friendlier.

Harry rescued the princess
and married her. Even Percy
was invited to their wedding.

The invitation said: "Please
come – but take a bath first!"

Try these other books in
Series One:

Wizards: One wizard looks after
orphans, one sells cures and one must
stop a band of robbers.

Giants: Two huge stories – about a
kind giant called a troll and how
three mean giants meet a grisly end.

Witches: Three bewitching tales:
one witch loses her broomstick,
another loses her temper, and the third
loses her cool with a clever farmer.

Dragons: Stan must outwit a
dragon to feed his children, while
Victor must persuade two dragons not
to eat him.

Designed by
Katarina Dragoslavić

First published in 2003 by Usborne Publishing Ltd., Usborne House,
83-85 Saffron Hill, London EC1N 8RT, England. www.usborne.com
Copyright © 2003, 1980 Usborne Publishing Ltd.